THE SECRET SEDER

By **DOREEN RAPPAPORT**

Illustrated by
EMILY ARNOLD McCULLY

HYPERION BOOKS FOR CHILDREN

NEW YORK

Text copyright © 2005 by Doreen Rappaport
Illustrations copyright © 2005 by Emily Arnold McCully

Printed in Singapore
This book was set in CG Cloister.

First Edition
3 5 7 9 10 8 6 4 2
Reinforced binding
Library of Congress Cataloging-in-Publication Data on file.
ISBN 0-7868-0777-6
Visit www.hyperionbooksforchildren.com

For Grandpa Sam
and Madison and Olivia
and Samara and Stella—D.R.

I AM WALKING as fast as I can. I have to get home and practice with Mama one last time. I want to run, but Papa says I must never run. It makes people stare.

When I get to the cathedral, I slow down. People on either side of me are crossing themselves as a sign of respect. I cross myself, too. It's dangerous not to. Everyone in the village thinks we're Catholics. But we're only pretending to be. We're really Jews.

There's a war going on. Germany is trying to conquer all of Europe. Last year Adolf Hitler's black-boot men came to Paris and took the Jews away. Papa and Mama and I escaped in the dark of night. Grandmama and Grandpapa ran away too, but we don't know where they went. Every day I pray that they are safe.

We got out of Paris, but we're still in danger. There are black-boot men here, too.

"Do we have time to practice, Mama?" Mama has been teaching me the Four Questions so I can surprise Papa at the Seder.

"Yes," she answers and looks away.

"*Ma nishtanah ha-lailah ha-zeh mi-kol ha-laylot?*" I whisper the Hebrew words. It's too dangerous to say them out loud. Mama says the walls have ears.

Usually Mama kisses Papa when he comes home from work. Today she doesn't even look up. "What's the matter?" Papa asks.

"They took Mr. Leclerc and his wife and son away today," she whispers.

Mr. Leclerc? I didn't even know he was Jewish.

"Étienne, it's too dangerous to take Jacques to the Seder," Mama says.

Papa takes Mama's hands in his. "Just being a Jew is dangerous," he answers.

"Mama, please," I plead. "We promised Grandpapa that we would celebrate all the holidays, no matter what."

Her eyes fill with tears. Papa wipes them away. "We'll be all right," he whispers.

Mama pulls me tight to her. She stuffs a roasted egg into my coat pocket. Papa slips a knife into his.

We walk down our street. When we near Mr. Leclerc's house, I walk faster. Papa pulls me back. "Walk naturally so we don't look suspicious," he whispers.

My feet slow up, but my heart still races.

We turn one corner, then another, then another. I hear clicking on the cobblestones behind us. Papa yanks me into an alley. The clicking is closer and louder. Papa pulls out the knife. I hold my breath. The clicking fades away, but my ears still ring.

At the edge of the village, we start up the mountain. The thick pines along the path block out the light. But I am not afraid of the darkness, only of the black-boot men.

Up, up, we climb. The only sound is the wind. Up, up. Suddenly I hear rustling in the forest. I stop and listen more carefully. The rustling is still there. Is someone following us?

Papa seems to read my mind. "It's probably a rabbit," he says.

I hope he is right.

We trudge on. Something snaps at my chest. I jump. So does my heart.

"It's only a branch of a small bush," Papa says.

But I still feel scared.

Finally we reach the top of the mountain. Two men are chopping wood near a shack. Papa walks over to them. How does he know they are friends? He whispers to them, and they open the door of the shack. It is cold and damp inside. Strange faces are crowded around a small table. No one says hello. No one even looks at us. Some men have their coat collars up over their heads. They sway and pray in Hebrew.

I put Mama's roasted egg on the table. The Seder table looks so empty. There is only a glowing candle, a bottle of wine, two cups, and one piece of matzah. I close my eyes and see Grandmama's Seder table last year, with the fancy lace cloth and silver so shiny I saw my face in it. I see her beautiful Seder plate, with all the foods. I feel Grandpapa tickling me before he lit the candles. I want them here.

Papa pulls his coat collar up over his head and takes me under. We sway as he chants. His chanting turns to gasping, then to sobbing. I hear other men sobbing, too. I hug Papa's leg. *Papa, please don't cry.*

"*Chers amis*, let us come together now," someone says.

We come out from the coat. An old man with dark circles under his eyes pours the first of four cups of wine.

"This is a dark time for our people," the old man says. "We are separated from our families and live in secret as Jews. Our Seder table is almost empty, but still we may renew our spirit as we celebrate Passover, when God delivered our people to freedom." He says a blessing in Hebrew. He drinks some wine, then passes the cup around. Papa lets me sip some. It tingles on my tongue.

"We have no bitter herbs to dip in salted water," says the old man.

"We do not need bitter herbs," says a deep voice. "Our lives are bitter enough."

No one speaks for a few minutes.

The old man reads from ragged sheets of paper. "It was spring when the Passover took place. Our ancestors were slaves in Egypt. Remember their tears when they were slaves, and remember the tears of all who are not free today."

The old man continues: "We have only one piece of matzah instead of the traditional three pieces." He puts half in his pocket and winks at me.

Grandpapa winked at me before he hid the matzah, too. Seder leaders always hide a piece of matzah, and the children "steal" it back. After the meal, the leader has to find it or pay a ransom. It's like a game.

I am the only child here, so I must play the game. I slip my hand into his pocket and take out the matzah. He pretends not to see me.

"*Ha lachmá anya di achalu . . .*" He holds up the other half of the matzah. "This is the bread of affliction. When our ancestors fled Egypt, they took bread that was sunbaking on the rocks with them. It had not yet risen." He sips more wine, then looks toward me.

"He doesn't know the Four Questions yet," Papa says.

"I *do* know them, Papa," I say proudly. "I practiced with Mama."

Papa's eyes widen in surprise and happiness.

"*Ma nishtanah ha-lailah ha-zeh mi-kol ha-laylot?* Why is this night different from all other nights?" I chant. "*She-b'chol ha-laylot anu ochlin chametz u-matzah.* . . . Because on all other nights we eat bread or matzah. On this night we eat only matzah. A second reason tonight is different is—"

The deep voice interrupts me. "I think tonight is different because tonight all over Europe, Jews are being murdered."

"It is not much different from when Pharaoh worked our people to death," Papa says.

"It is not much different from when our people were expelled from Spain and Portugal," says another man.

"It *is* different," insists the deep voice. "For hundreds are being murdered every day, and thousands more will be murdered if Hitler is not stopped."

Again there is silence.

Then the old man nods at me, and I finish the questions. "Good work, my son," he says.

Papa hugs me.

The old man tells our people's history, starting from Abraham's time. He is a good storyteller, like Grandpapa.

Suddenly, the door bursts open. I grab for Papa's hand and squeeze my eyes shut, afraid to see who it is.

"It's all right," Papa whispers. "It is only one of the men who was chopping wood. He was keeping watch outside. Now he's come to hear part of the Seder."

The old man continues: "The *Haggadah* says that a long time ago five learned rabbis sat around a Seder table as we do now. They told and retold the story of our people's flight from Egypt into the Holy Land, searching for its meaning." He lowers his voice. "It was dangerous for them to do this, for they were forbidden to study or teach their religion."

"It is dangerous for us to do this too," I say. I am surprised at my voice.

He finishes the story of Passover. "Pharaoh was so cruel to our people that they cried out to God for help. God sent Moses to tell Pharaoh to free them. Pharaoh refused. Then God brought ten plagues upon the Egyptians so Pharaoh would see His power and determination to help the Israelites."

He dips my pinky into the cup of wine. "Blood spilling over Egypt . . . Frogs spilling out over the waters in Egypt . . . Lice . . ." Each time he names one of the plagues, I dip my pinky into the wine and put a droplet of it on the table.

His voice quivers when he gets to the tenth and final plague. "And God told Pharaoh He would kill all first-born sons in Egypt, including the animals. He told the Hebrews to wipe the blood of a slaughtered lamb over their doorposts, so that He would know to pass over their houses. And when the first-born were slain, Pharaoh finally freed the Israelites."

"Why doesn't He free us?" someone moans, then disappears under his coat.

"Tonight we *are* free," Papa says. "We are free inside ourselves, for by celebrating Pesach, we defy orders not to practice our religion."

There is another prayer, then more wine, then another prayer. Then we sing, "*Day-day-eynu, Day-day-eynu, Day-day-eynu . . .*" We do not sing out loud. We whisper-sing. We move our hands in rhythm to the words. We sway our bodies back and forth. Everyone is smiling, even the man with the deep voice. I feel happy to be here, happy that we are all together.

"Remember God's promise to guide and protect our ancestors and their descendants," says the old man. He points to the matzah. "Remember that our people left Egypt so quickly that the bread sunbaking on the rocks had no time to rise." He talks about the missing ceremonial foods, and I can see them on the table.

"*Baruch atah, Adonai, Eloheynu melech ha-olam, ha-motzi lechem min ha'aretz.* In this ugly time, it is easy to lose faith," he says. "Let us eat this matzah for strength." We pass it around until there are only crumbs left.

"In normal times," he says, "we would now sit down and eat a big meal with our families." He pauses. "Usually, *too* big."

I see Grandpapa dipping his spoon into Grandmama's chicken soup and scooping up part of a matzah ball.

"But tonight we can't. I—I—" the old man stammers. His hands tremble. The ragged papers in his hands drop to the floor. His whole body is shaking now. He looks like he is going to faint. I take the matzah out from my pocket and put it in his hands.

He nods his thanks and pats my head.

The fourth cup of wine is poured, and a cup for the Prophet Elijah. The old man calls out to God, "Pour your wrath upon the nations that do not recognize you. . . ." I open the door for Elijah. A cold blast of wind sweeps through the cabin. No one speaks as we listen to the wind.

The deep voice breaks the silence. "Next year, in *Yerushalayim*, we shall come together for a great feast," he says.

"Next year in *Yerushalayim*." We whisper these beautiful words and hug each other good-bye. The wind whips around us as we go our separate ways. I take Papa's hand, and we begin our walk down the mountain.

ABOUT THIS BOOK

From 1939 to 1945, more than six million Jews and three million other Europeans considered "undesirable" by Germany's leader Adolf Hitler were murdered or died of starvation and disease in work camps and concentration camps. One and a half million were Jewish children. We call this terrible time in history the Holocaust, or *Shoah*.

Pesach is the Hebrew word for Passover. Passover, or the Festival of Freedom, celebrates liberation and rebirth. It lasts for eight nights and eight days. On the first two nights, Jews gather together at a Seder. (Reform Jews celebrate one Seder and observe the holiday for seven nights and seven days.) Seder means "order." A Seder is not just the retelling of the story of the Israelites' journey from freedom to slavery. It helps people experience the bitterness of slavery and the sweetness of freedom. The Passover story had great meaning for Jews trying to survive during the *Shoah*.

Some Jews managed to run away and hide until the war was over. More than 10,000 Jewish partisans in hiding formed their own fighting units against the Germans. More than 25,000 Jewish partisans joined forces with the Soviet Army.

Some Jewish families were hidden by Christian families. Children were hidden in convents, orphanages, haylofts, and cellars. Some hidden Jews took new names and passed as Christians. The "black-boot" men that Jacques is afraid of could be German or French; for unfortunately, some French people collaborated with the Nazis and turned in their Jewish neighbors.

This story was inspired by real events. Even with guns firing during the uprising in the Warsaw Ghetto, some Jews celebrated Passover. Vladka Meed, living outside the Warsaw Ghetto as a Christian, wrote about celebrating Passover in *On Both Sides of the Wall: Memoirs of the Warsaw Ghetto. (Lohame Ha-Getaot/*Ghetto Fighters' House, 1972). Nechama Tec wrote that Jews hiding in Poland's forests held Seders without ceremonial foods in *Defiance: The Bielski Partisans* (New York, Oxford University Press, 1993). At a Seder in Vilna, Poland, a fourteen-year-old resistance fighter asked the Four Questions, which sparked an intense discussion on the meaning of Passover (Rick Cohen: *The Avengers: A Jewish Story*. New York: Alfred A. Knopf, 2000). Hiding in a French village, a Belgian Jew named Bernard Mednicki took his son to a Seder in the mountains and wrote about it in *Never Be Afraid: A Jew in the Maquis* (Mica Press: Madison, Wisconsin, 1997, coauthored with Ken Wachsberger).

I remain overwhelmed by the hideous statistics of the Holocaust, and in awe of the faith of so many Jews despite their brutal and demoralizing circumstances in the face of death. I hope this book helps you understand their courage and determination and the courage and determination of all people throughout history who refused to renounce their beliefs despite the threat of death.

I thank Rabbi Burt Schuman, Temple Beth Israel, Altoona, Pennsylvania; Dr. Alan Berger, Eminent Scholar of Holocaust Studies, Florida Atlantic University; and Dr. Barry Mesch, Hebrew College, for critiquing the manuscript. I also thank a most special reader, Kevin Cote, who keeps me honest and in touch with what children do or do not understand.

MORE ABOUT PASSOVER

The Seder plate contains symbolic foods:

THE *BAYTZAH* (bay-TZAH), the roasted egg, symbolizes the festival offerings in ancient times and springtime.

CHAROSET or *HAROSET* (kha-RO-set), a mixture of apples, nuts, wine, and spices, symbolizes the bricks and mortar the Israelites were forced to make for the Egyptians.

THE *CHAZERET* (kha-ZEH-ret) or vegetables such as lettuce, watercress, radish, or any vegetable that tends to be or become bitter, has the same symbolism as the *maror*.

KARPAS (kar-PAS) are the fresh greens that symbolize springtime and rebirth.

MAROR (ma-ROAR), a bitter herb like horseradish, symbolizes the bitter lot of the enslaved Israelites.

ZEROA (ze-ro-AH), the roasted bone, symbolizes the lamb the Israelites roasted and ate on the night they left Egypt.

IF YOU WANT TO LEARN MORE ABOUT PASSOVER:

Diamond Goldin, Barbara. *The Passover Journey: A Seder Companion*. Illustrated by Neil Waldman. New York: Viking Penguin, 1994.

Manushkin, Fran. *The Matzah That Papa Brought Home*. Illustrated by Ned Bittinger. New York: Scholastic, Inc., 2001.

Rush, Barbara, and Cherie Karo Schwartz. *The Kids' Catalog of Passover: A Worldwide Celebration*. Philadelphia: Jewish Publication Society, 1999.

Schecter, Ellen. *The Family Haggadah*. Illustrated by Neil Waldman. New York: Viking Children's Books, 1999.

Schilder, Rosalind. *DAYENU or How Uncle Murray Saved the Seder*. Illustrated by Katherine Janus Kahn. Rockville, Maryland: Kar-Ben Copies, Inc., 1988.

Sper, Emily. *Passover Seder*. New York: Scholastic Inc., 2003.

IF YOU WANT TO LEARN MORE ABOUT THE EXPERIENCES
OF CHILDREN DURING THE HOLOCAUST:

Adler, David. *Hiding from the Nazis*. Illustrated by Karen Ritz. New York: Holiday House, 1997.

———. *Hilde and Eli: Children of the Holocaust*. Illustrated by Karen Ritz. New York: Holiday House, 1994.

Bunting, Eve. *One Candle*. Illustrated by K. Wendy Popp. New York: HarperCollins Children's Books, 2002.

Frank, Anne. *Anne Frank: The Diary of a Young Girl*. New York: Bantam Books, 1993.

Oppenheim, Shulamith Levey. *The Lily Cupboard*. Illustrated by Ronald Himler. New York: Harper and Row, 1992.

Polacco, Patricia. *The Butterfly*. New York: Putnam, 2000.

Rosenberg, Maxine. *Hiding to Survive: Stories of Jewish Children Rescued from the Holocaust*. New York: Clarion Books, 1994.